To Sadie and Eli:
meet you in the closet, cha cha cha
—R. P.

Library of Congress Cataloging-in-Publication Data Available

10   9   8   7   6   5   4   3   2

Published by Sterling Publishing Co., Inc.

387 Park Avenue South, New York, NY 10016

Text copyright © 2005 by Robin Parnell

Illustrations copyright © 2005 by Jimmy Pickering

Designed by Donna Mark

Distributed in Canada by Sterling Publishing

c/o Canadian Manda Group, 165 Dufferin Street

Toronto, Ontario, Canada M6K 3H6

Distributed in Great Britain and Europe by Chris Lloyd at Orca Book

Services, Stanley House, Fleets Lane, Poole BH15 3AJ, England

Distributed in Australia by Capricorn Link (Australia) Pty. Ltd.

P.O. Box 704, Windsor, NSW 2756, Australia

Printed in China

Sterling ISBN 1-4027-1298-7

For information about custom editions, special sales, premium and

corporate purchases, please contact Sterling Special Sales

Department at 800-805-5489 or specialsales@sterlingpub.com

MY CLOSET THREW A PARTY

Robyn Parnell

**Illustrated by
Jimmy Pickering**

Sterling Publishing Co., Inc.
New York

My closet threw a party
and I heard it was a hit!
The clean clothes mixed with stinky
and my pants danced till they split.

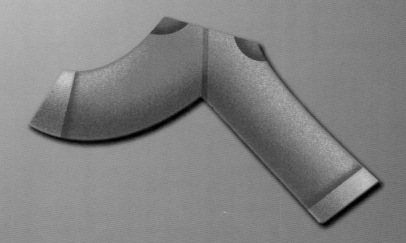

Raincoat mentioned with great cheer,
"It was the blowout of the year!
It was fabulous, I swear ...
Simply everyone was there!"

My stockings swung from shades . . .

. . . while my sneakers played charades.

Then my purple paisley pants
asked the laundry bag to dance!

And my checkered flannel nightie
that I hang upon the hook
did a cheerful kind of cha-cha
when she thought no one would look.

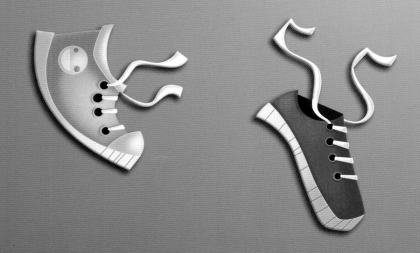

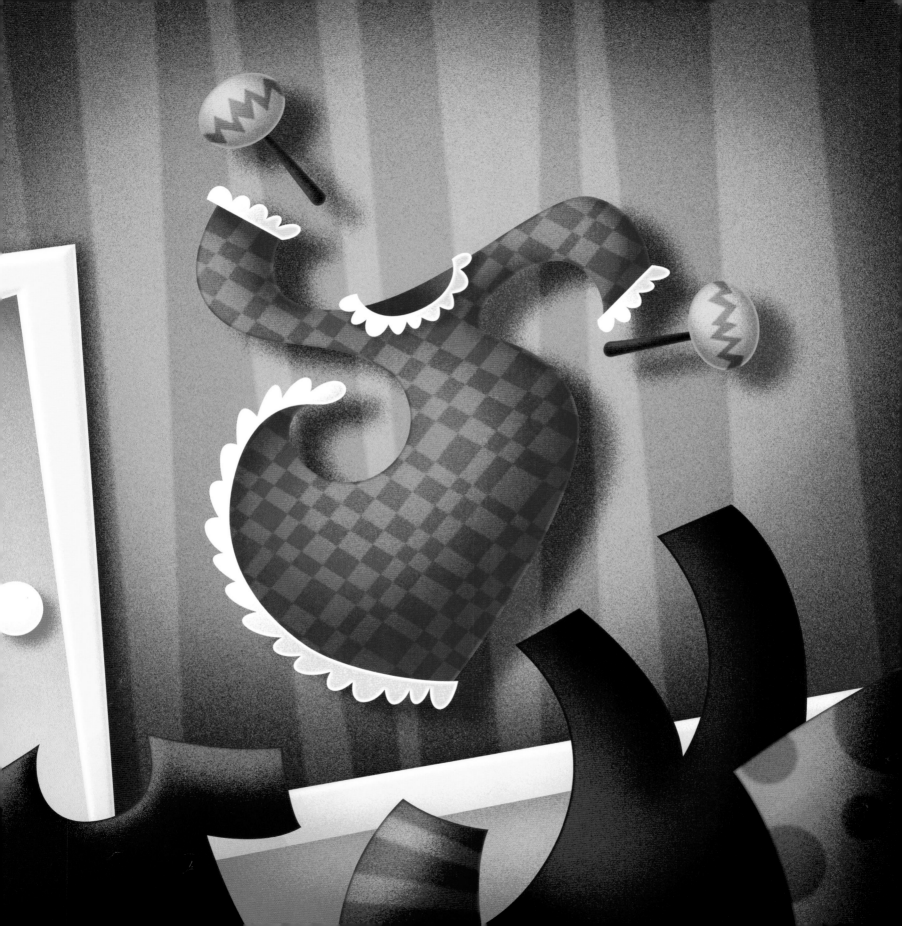

It was really quite a sight,
starting early in the night.
"And they partied on till three!"
cried my jubilant shoe tree.

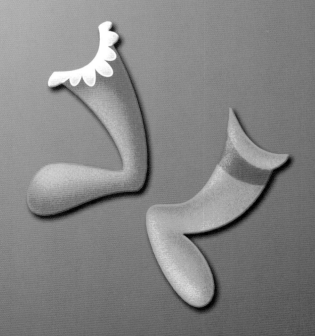

But just then I heard a stirring
from outside my bedroom door . . .

It was Mom—oh dear!—what could I do?

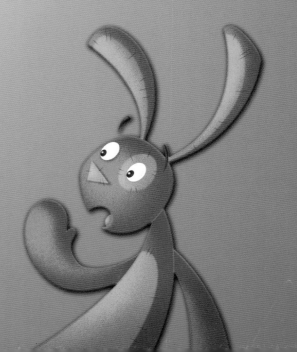

My room was on the floor!

Well, I can't believe I wasn't there
to see a sweater disco on my chair.